EGMONT

We bring stories to life

This edition published in Great Britain in 2008
by Dean an imprint of Egmont UK Limited
239 Kensington High Street, London W8 6SA
© 2008 Disney Enterprises, Inc
Based on the Winnie-the-Pooh works by A. A. Milne and E. H. Shepard
Illustrations by Andrew Grey
Text by Laura Dollin

ISBN 978 0 6035 6359 1
1 3 5 7 9 10 8 6 4 2
Printed in China

All About

Piglet

This book belongs to . . .

Meet Piglet

Piglet may be a Very Small Animal, but he has a **big** heart. Known to be a tiny bit Anxious sometimes, he tries very hard with everything he does, especially when practising writing his own name,

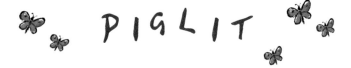

PIGLIT

Being small, Piglet likes to have Company. This often means holding Winnie-the-Pooh's paw (just to be sure of him), for Pooh is his very best friend.

In this book, you too can keep Piglet company and learn all about some of his Big Adventures (**Big** for one quite so Small).

A Poem about Piglet

Piglet is Small
But that's not all:
His bravery shows
That when the wind blows
His dear friends mean more than ever before
As he battles his way through a bluster.

So what does he do?
With persuasion from Pooh,
He climbs up some string
(What a Very Grand Thing),
To go and fetch help (not so much as a yelp)
And save his dear friends from a fluster.

Facts about Piglet

He lives in the middle of everything.
Piglet lives in a grand house, in the middle of a beech-tree, which is in the middle of the Forest.

Piglet's grandfather was called Trespassers William. Next to Piglet's house is a board with "TRESPASSERS W" written on it (short for Trespassers William), which Piglet thinks was his grandfather's name.

Sometimes Piglet feels very afraid, for it is hard to be brave when you're only a Very Small Animal. But sometimes being small makes him very Useful, and when one's very Useful, one forgets to be frightened.

Piglet thinks he saw a heffalump once, but he's not sure. Perhaps it wasn't, after all.

Piglet has never been fond of baths. He would much rather be a muddy colour. So Piglet is most anxious indeed when Kanga suggests a COLD bath when he is pretending to be Roo.

Piglet can be very Brave, such as the time he escaped through Owl's letterbox to fetch help when Owl's tree fell down. Pooh promised him it would be a Very Grand Thing to talk about afterwards.

 **Piglet is an excitable fellow,** especially when tracking Woozles with Pooh (or indeed Wizzles).

Thoughtful and kind, giving presents is what Piglets do best. Like the balloon he gave to cheer up gloomy Eeyore.

Piglet tried flying, but didn't really take to it.

In which we read about

Piglet

One sunny afternoon, when Piglet, Winnie-the-Pooh and Christopher Robin were enjoying a friendly talk together, Christopher Robin happened to say,

"Piglet, I saw a heffalump today".

Piglet felt a little uneasy, but wanted to sound as if
he knew what Christopher Robin was talking about.

"I saw one once," he replied. "At least, I think I did."

By and by, Piglet and Pooh decided it was time to go home and walked side-by-side through the Forest.

After a moment, Pooh said solemnly, "Piglet, I have decided something."

"What's that, Pooh?"

"I have decided to catch a heffalump,"

he declared.

Piglet said nothing, but only because he rather wished *he* had come up with the idea first.

However, soon he had forgotten his disappointment and set about helping Pooh work out how to trap a heffalump. It seemed that digging a Very Deep Pit would be a good start; a deep pit very near a heffalump so that the heffalump might fall into it quite quickly. Pooh and Piglet then wondered how one might keep the heffalump there once trapped . . .

"Supposing you wanted to catch *me*," pondered Pooh, "how would *you* go about it?"

Piglet thought for a moment and then explained that he would make a Trap with honey inside it so that Pooh would smell it and go after it.

And so, before Pooh became too lost in his
dreams of that sticky honey smell,
Piglet sent him to fetch some
honey while he set about
digging the deep pit.

Pooh went home to find only one pot of honey
left on his shelf. *Surely* he had some more?
Oh well, never mind.
This would have to do, he thought.

A little while later, Pooh returned with a honey pot.
He passed it down to Piglet who was at the bottom
of the pit.

"Is that all you had left?" Piglet said, peering into
the jar. Pooh had to confess that he'd eaten some of the
honey, just to make sure that it *was* honey and
not anything else – cheese perhaps.

Piglet left the jar at the bottom of the Pit and the
two friends said goodnight, agreeing to meet early the
following morning to see how many heffalumps
they had caught in the trap.

That night, Pooh woke up suddenly with a funny
feeling in his tummy. He knew what that funny feeling
meant – he was HUGRY! So he went to the
larder and reached up for a jar of honey. But he found
NOTHING. Pooh was rather muddled and
walked up and down, murmuring a murmur in
a puzzled sort of
way, before he
remembered that
he had put his last
pot of honey into
the Trap to catch
a heffalump.
"Bother!"
he said, and went
back to bed.

But Pooh couldn't
sleep and after trying
Counting Sheep,
he tried counting
heffalumps.

But that was no good either. He jumped out of bed
and ran straight to the spot where the Very Deep Pit
had been dug.

There, at the bottom, was his jar of honey. And
although he had already eaten most of it there was a
little left at the very bottom of the jar.

He pushed his head into the jar and began to lick . . .

Meanwhile, Piglet woke up, his mind still a bit
of a whirl with heffalump wonderings. Like . . .
"What if heffalumps didn't like pigs very
much?" and other such worrying thoughts.

He comforted himself with the knowledge
that Pooh would be with him, but perhaps
heffalumps didn't like Bears either . . .

He decided to be brave and check the Trap for heffalumps. Off he went, muttering "Oh, dear, oh, dear, oh, dear!" as he did so. When he reached the trap, he peered in.

At that moment, a loud roaring noise arose from the Pit and Piglet, as frightened as a little pig can be, scampered away.

"*Help, help!*" he cried. "A Herrible Hoffalump! *Help!* A Hoffable Hellerump!" And he didn't stop until he got to Christopher Robin's house.

"Whatever's the matter, Piglet?" asked Christopher Robin. Piglet explained about the heffalump and how it had the biggest head you *ever* saw, like an enormous jar . . .

Christopher Robin agreed to come and look at it. He, too, could hear something as they got near the Pit. Then he began to laugh. And he laughed and laughed and laughed . . .

The terrible noise was Pooh,

with his head stuck in the jar,

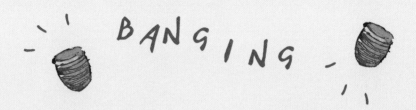

BANGING

against a tree-root.

At that moment, his head popped out, and, on seeing Pooh Bear (not a heffalump), Piglet realised what a silly animal he'd been.

He felt so very silly that he ran straight home to bed with a headache, while Christopher Robin and Pooh shared a loving chuckle before setting off to have breakfast together.

Not long after Piglet's adventure with the
heffalump Trap, the Hundred Acre Wood was
a very wet place to be, for it rained and rained
and rained.

One morning, little Piglet looked out of his
window and wished that he'd had Company all this
time, for then at least he might have had a jolly
time talking with Pooh or Christopher Robin
about it. After all, it was quite exciting to see such
a flood. But Piglet did feel a little Anxious.

"Pooh could escape by
Climbing Trees," he thought,
"Kanga could Jump, Owl
could fly . . . and here am
I surrounded by water and
I can't do anything."

Still it rained and rained, and every day the water got higher, until it was nearly up to Piglet's window. It was at this point that Piglet decided he should do something, and he thought and thought of what that something might be. Then he remembered that Christopher Robin had told him a story about a man on a desert island who wrote a message in a bottle before throwing it into the sea. *That's* what he would do! Then perhaps someone might find the bottle and come to rescue him.

So he found a bottle and some paper and a pencil, then he wrote:

HELP!
PIGLIT (ME)

before putting the paper in the bottle and corking the bottle tightly.

He leaned out of the window as far as he could
without falling into the water and dropped the bottle
with a splash! Watching it bob away into the distance, he
hoped someone would find it very soon. Then he sighed
a long sigh and wished that his friend Pooh was there
because it was so very much more friendly with two.

Meanwhile, Pooh Bear woke up after a very long sleep to find his house was flooded and his feet were wet.

"This is Serious," he said to himself. And with that, he took his **biggest** pot of honey and escaped with it to a large branch of his tree.

Then he climbed down to get the next pot of honey, and the next one after that, and the next one after that . . . until his Escape was complete and Pooh was sitting on the branch with ten pots of honey beside him.

One by one, he ate them all and it was while enjoying the last sticky mouthful of the last pot of honey that he noticed Piglet's bottle floating past him. With only one thing on his mind, he plunged into the water with a loud cry of "Honey!"

But it soon became clear no honey was inside.

"Bother!" said Pooh. Then he saw the piece of paper. He took it out and pondered upon it for a moment.

"Hmmm," he said. "It's a Missage. That's what it is . . . and that letter is a 'P' and 'P' means 'Pooh'." He decided to find Christopher Robin or Owl to help him read it.

Being a Bear who couldn't swim, Pooh realised he would have to find another way to get to them. An idea came to him, one he was rather pleased about (being a Bear of Very Little Brain):

"If a bottle can float," he said to himself, "a jar can float, and if it's a big enough jar, I can sit on top of it."

So he took his biggest jar and made it watertight. Naming his new found vessel *The Floating Bear*, he set off, bobbing up and down a bit, just managing to paddle through the rainwater.

It was just about this moment in time, that in another part of the Wood, Christopher Robin bumped into Owl. Together they were wondering whether Pooh and Piglet were all right in these rainy conditions and just as Christopher Robin began to worry about his lovable Bear, a growly voice behind him said,

"Hello, I'm here!"

Christopher Robin was so pleased to see Pooh
that he gave him a huge hug.

Pooh proudly showed him his boat and then the
Very Important Missage in the bottle.

"It's from Piglet!" cried Christopher Robin,
reading the message (it was then that Pooh realised
the "Ps" were for "Piglet" and not for "Pooh").

"We must rescue him!" said Pooh.

With that, he
sent Owl off
to tell Piglet
that Rescue
was on
its way.

By now, Piglet was beginning to think that
perhaps he might *never* be rescued and that he
would try hard to be very brave.

So he was most grateful to see Owl,
when he arrived to tell him of the coming Rescue,
although the Rescue didn't come soon enough
for poor Piglet, who had to listen to Owl's very
long story about an aunt who laid a seagull's egg
by mistake.

Feeling very tired, Piglet began to fall asleep and
it was only a loud

from Owl that woke him with a start and stopped
him falling out of the window into the water.

You can therefore imagine his joy and relief when he saw Christopher Robin and Pooh floating towards him in an *umbrella!* (Pooh had astounded even Christopher Robin with his clever umbrella idea).

At last, he was being rescued! Once again, he could be with his *dearest* friend, Pooh Bear and enjoy some Company.

And that is the end of Piglet's Big Adventure in the rain — an adventure in which, I think you'll agree, he was a Very Brave Piglet.

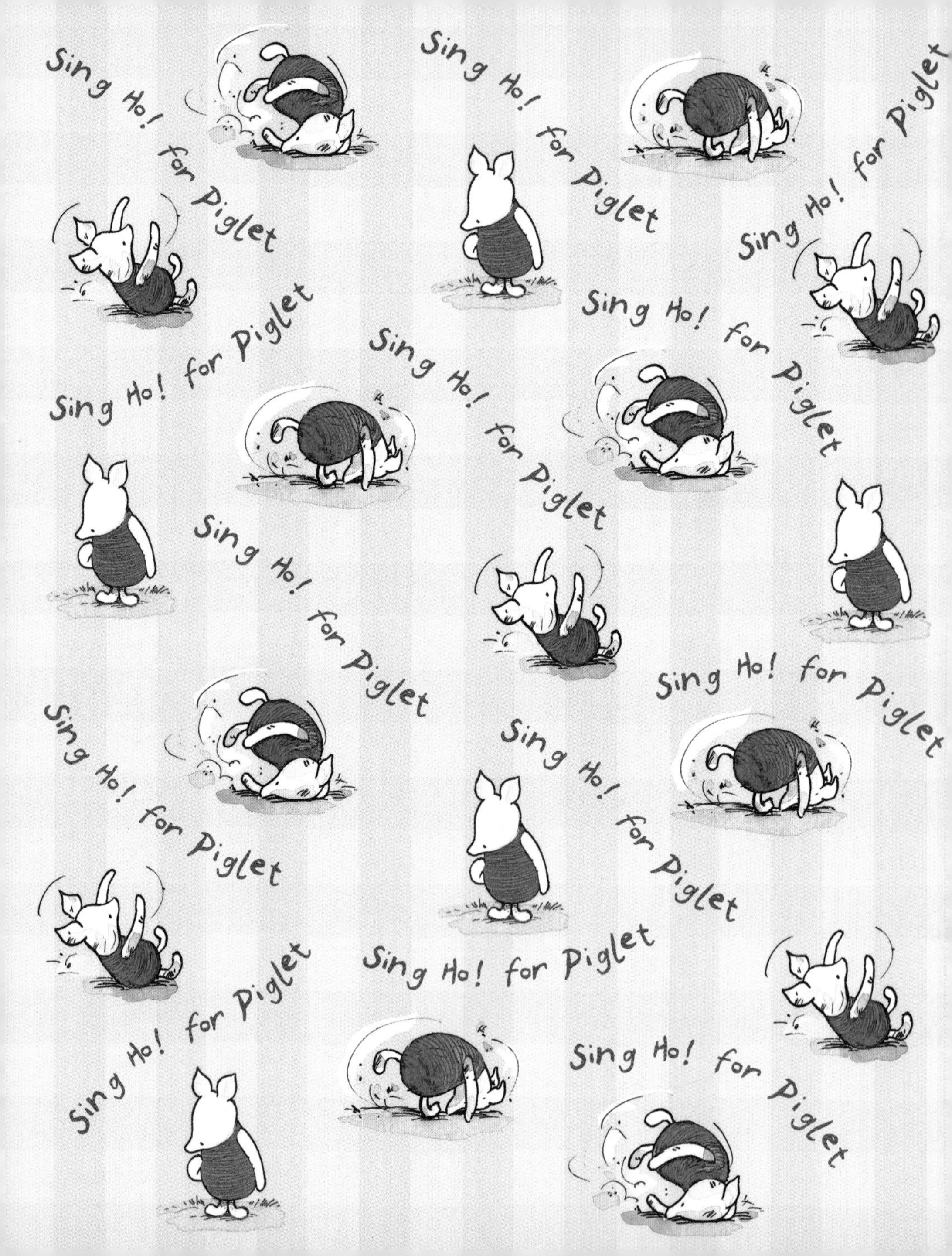
Sing Ho! for Piglet